Where Is He?
Copyright © 2022 by Parimalasri Docktor

All rights reserved. No part of this publication may be reproduced, distributed, or transmitted in any form or by any means, including photocopying, recording, or other electronic or mechanical methods, without the prior written permission of the author, except in the case of brief quotations embodied in critical reviews and certain other non-commercial uses permitted by copyright law.

Tellwell Talent
www.tellwell.ca

ISBN
978-0-2288-6860-6 (Hardcover)
978-0-2288-6859-0 (Paperback)
978-0-2288-6861-3 (eBook)

Where Is He?
Tank, the tortoise

Parimalasri Docktor

Illustrated by Floyd Ryan Yamyamin

"I am waiting," Tank thought to himself. "Where is he? It is time for my bath and my favorite meal, string beans. Where is he?" It felt like tortoise years until Tank heard a click at the door.

"Finally, he is here!" thought Tank, but the voice was different. That was not Mr. Bean's voice. Mr. Bean's voice was a little raspy and slow. Things were moved around.

Tank heard a lot of noise. A huge hand scooped Tank up and placed him in a box that Tank was able to see through.

He saw a picture of Mr. Bean right next to his box. Tank remembered Mr. Bean's face even in his sweet dreams. Every day, Mr. Bean always looked Tank in the eye after a nice bath and kissed his beak.

Then, Mr. Bean always fed Tank string beans. Tank always felt so happy that he wagged his tail.

Tank was taken to a place where many people visited every day. This was a pet store. At the pet store, Tank was placed in a glass box.

In his box, there was a log that he could hide under.

One dish had water, and another dish had lettuce and pellets. Tank was not used to that food.

He wondered to himself, "Where is he?" He was very hungry, so he ate some lettuce. He preferred beans.

A woman stopped at the store from time to time. The store clerk said to her, "Tank's owner died, and we do not know how old this Russian tortoise is. He doesn't move around much. He just sits and waits. Maybe he is thinking that his owner will come."

Tank missed his routine. Tank missed Mr. Bean.

Two months passed, and the woman stopped by at the pet store. Tank was still there. He looked like he had lost some weight.

One day, the woman decided to bring her husband to the store. Tank was still there. Tank ate some lettuce and looked around to see the visitors.

As soon as Tank heard the man's voice, he came out from under the log.

He thought to himself, "That voice sounds like Mr. Bean's voice. But maybe it is not him. This man's voice is a little louder."

The man gently took Tank in his hands and kissed his beak and said, "You are coming home." Tank remembered that Mr. Bean always kissed his beak.

When Tank arrived at his new home, he had a nice warm soak in the tub and guess what?

After his bath, he was fed string beans!
He was too full to finish his meal.

Tank thought to himself, "I am home. He is here."

That night, for the first time in months, he slept well.

CPSIA information can be obtained
at www.ICGtesting.com
Printed in the USA
LVHW070514020822
724957LV00011B/291